WINDMILL BOOKS

I Can Draw Wild Animals

Contents

Elephant

1. Draw a carrot shape to create a tusk.

2. Add the curved trunk, mouth, chin, and head.

3. Now you can add an oval-shaped ear.

4. Draw a rounded oval for the elephant's large body.

5. Draw four stout legs and some toenails.

6. Add a tail, water spray, and head and body details.

Dolphin

1. Draw a tear shape. Add fins and snout.

2. Add a line to the lower part of the body.

3. Draw a fin on the dolphin's back.

4. Sketch in the tail with its flukes.

5. Draw an eye, brow, and blowhole.

6. Finish by adding details and shading.

Fox

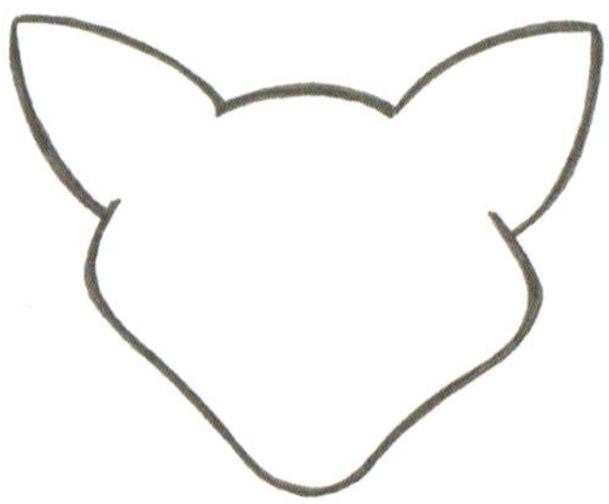

1. Draw a diamond shape. Add ears.

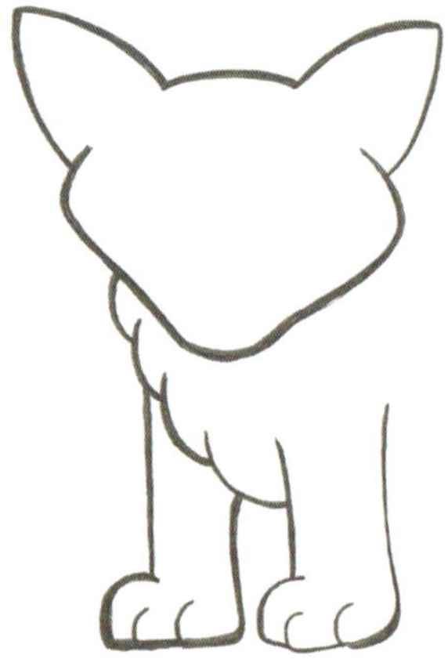

2. Pencil a furry chest, front legs, and paws.

3. Draw the tummy, hind legs, and back.

4. Give the fox a huge, fluffy tail.

5. Add whiskers, a nose, and eyes to the face.

6. Shade the nose and coat and add details to the ears.

Monkey

1. Draw an oval and a big smile.

2. Draw a half circle and inside it pencil an "m."

3. Add face features and hair strands to the head.

4. Draw an oval body and two legs and feet.

5. Now, add long arms and hands.

6. Finish with a long tail and some shading.

Flamingo

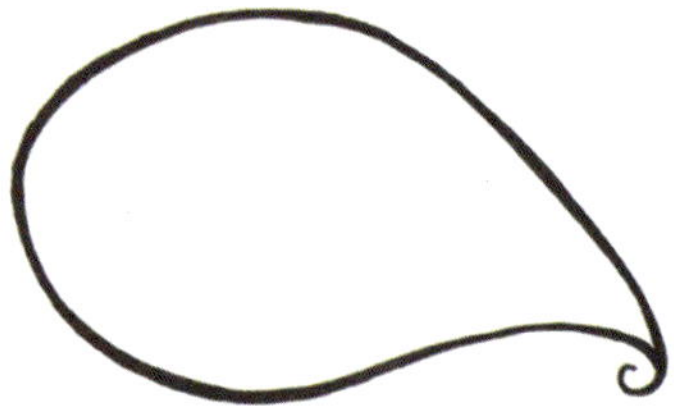

1. Draw the tear-shaped body.

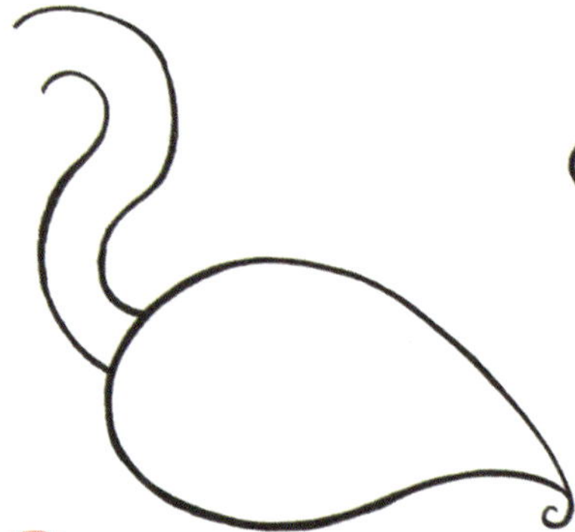

2. Add a long, curved neck.

3. Draw the head and large beak.

4. Pencil in a wing and add feathers.

5. Sketch in long, thin striped legs and feet.

6. Add face features and body details.

Giraffe

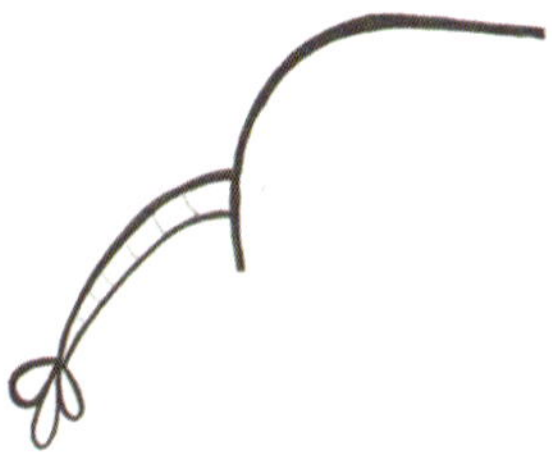

1. Draw the rump and tail.

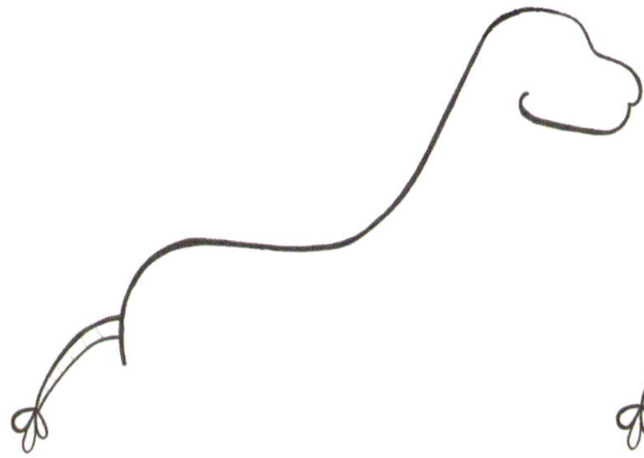

2. Sketch the back, neck, and head.

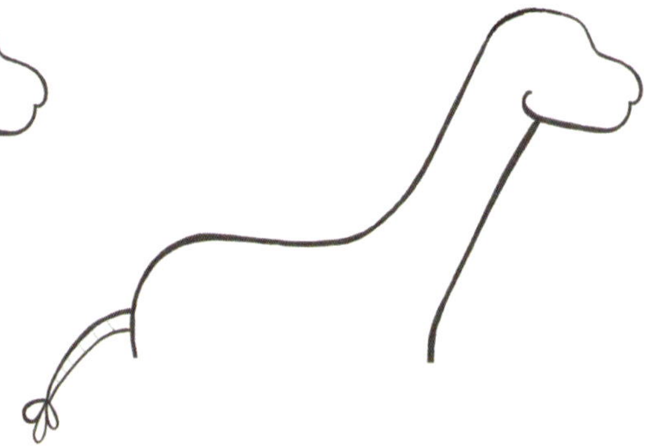

3. Now draw the rest of the giraffe's long neck.

4. Pencil two hoofed legs and the tummy.

5. Add the ear, eye, mouth, horns, and nostrils.

6. Draw the mane and sketch the coat pattern.

Owl

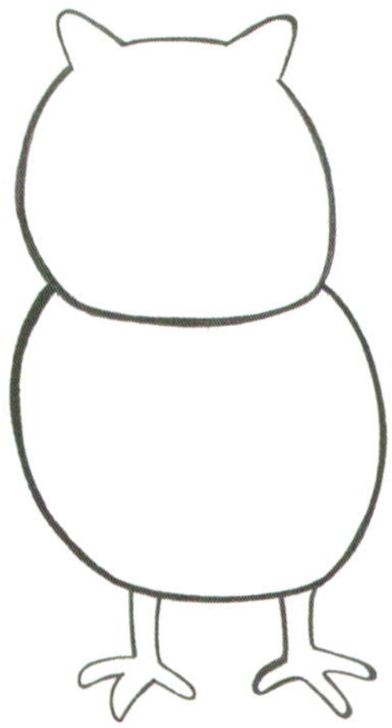

1. Draw a rough circle and add pointed ears.

2. Draw the body, legs, and clawed feet.

3. Draw a wing on each side of the body.

4. Sketch two large eyes and a sharp beak.

5. Mark the owl's chest with two lines.

6. Finish by adding shading and details.

Squirrel

1. Draw an oval and add ears.

2. Sketch the body. Add a furry chest and paws.

3. Draw eyes and hind legs and paws.

4. Add a nose, mouth, and two teeth to the face.

5. Now, give the squirrel a large, fluffy tail.

6. Finish by adding details and texture to the fur.

Kangaroo

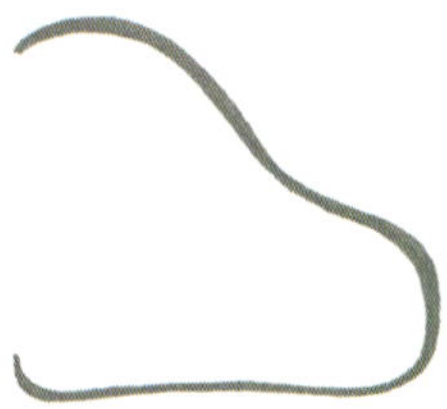

1. Draw a rounded triangular head.

2. Add the ears, eye, brow, and nostril to the face.

3. Sketch a curve for the kangaroo's back.

4. Draw the neck, chest, and one arm.

5. Add the tummy, hind leg, and a long foot.

6. Draw the other leg and foot and the tail.

Lion

1. Draw a circle for the head.

2. Pencil the ears, eyes, nose, and mouth.

3. Draw a large mane around the head.

4. Draw the front legs, paws, and chest.

5. Now add back legs and paws.

6. Add a tail and whiskers and shading.

Koala

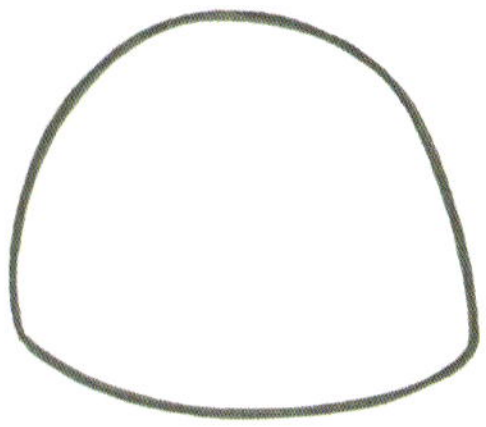

1. Draw a half circle for the head.

2. Add two large ears and a nose.

3. Pencil the eyes, brows, and mouth.

4. Sketch the furry body, a leg, and an arm.

5. Draw a branch, a second arm, and claws on the limbs.

6. Finish by adding detail to the ears and some shading.

Panda

1. Draw a circle. Add ears and eye patches.

2. Pencil a nose, mouth, eyes, and brows.

3. Draw in the panda's two front arms and hands.

4. Outline the back, chest, and tummy.

5. Draw two back legs and paws and a tail.

6. Shade part of the body and the eyes, ears, tail, and arms.

Hippo

1. Start by drawing the hippo's eyes.

2. Now draw the top of the head and the upper jaw.

3. Add two ears and two large teeth.

4. Outline the rounded back and chest.

5. Draw four legs and some toenails.

6. Add a little tail and wrinkles to the skin.

Frog

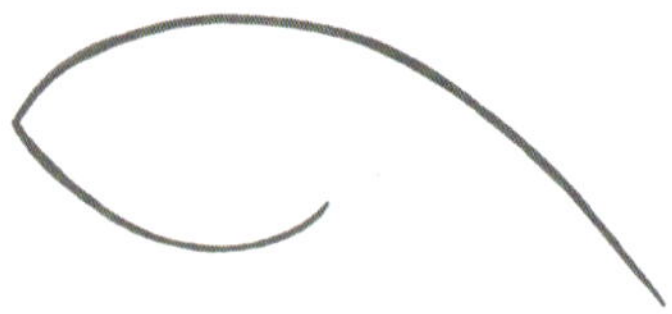

1. Draw a curved line to form the back and mouth.

2. Sketch the chest and a leg with long toes.

3. Create a back leg with two curved lines.

4. Draw a long-toed foot on the rear leg.

5. Pencil the tummy, second front leg, and a glimpse of the second back leg.

6. Draw huge eyes and add spots to the body.

Tiger

1. Draw the head, ears, and bearded muzzle.

2. Outline the tiger's back and long tail.

3. Draw the furry chest, front legs, and tummy.

4. Now sketch in the rear legs.

5. Add face features and fur to the front legs.

6. Finish with shaded stripes on the body.

Published in 2019 by Windmill Books,
an Imprint of Rosen Publishing
29 East 21st Street, New York, NY 10010

Created and Produced by Green Android Limited
Illustrations by Grace Sandford

Cataloging-in-Publication Data

Names: Sandford, Grace.
Title: I can draw wild animals / Grace Sandford.
Description: New York : Windmill Books, 2019. | Series: I can draw
Identifiers: ISBN 9781538390214 (pbk.) | ISBN 9781508197317 (library bound) | ISBN 9781538390221 (6 pack)
Subjects: LCSH: Animals in art--Juvenile literature. | Wildlife art--Juvenile literature. | Drawing--Technique--Juvenile literature.
Classification: LCC NC780.S264 2019 | DDC 743.6--dc23
Manufactured in the United States of America

CPSIA Compliance Information: Batch BW19WM: For Further Information contact Rosen Publishing, New York, New York at 1-800-237-9932